# Little Bo Peep
### and Her
# BAD, BAD SHEEP

A MOTHER GOOSE HULLABALOO

by A.L. Wegwerth
illustrated by Luke Flowers

CAPSTONE YOUNG READERS
a capstone imprint

Little Bo Peep . . .

Little Bo Peep
has lost her sheep—

**Come
BAAAACK!**

*Ahem!*
Little Bo Peep
has lost her sheep
and doesn't know where to find them—

# As I was saying,

Little Bo Peep
has lost her sheep
and doesn't know where to find them—

## HERE, BOY!

Does **anybody** want to hear this nursery rhyme?

# WHERE, OH WHERE, HAS MY LITTLE DOG GONE?

Fly's in the buttermilk, shoo, fly, shoo.

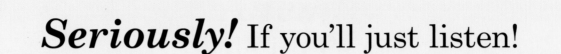

*Seriously!* If you'll just listen!

I can't see anything in this mess! Going by foot may be best.

# BINGO!!

You've **got** to be kidding me . . .

Oh, Mother Goose, my sheep are on the loose!

Little Bo Peep
has lost her sheep
and doesn't know where to find them.
Leave them alone,
and they'll come home,
wagging their tails behind them.

*(My sincerest apologies for the interruptions.*
*How could I get a word in with all that hullabaloo?)*

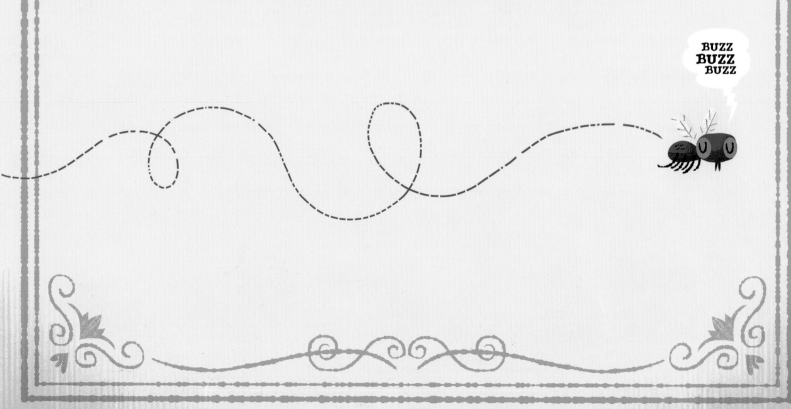

# DID YOU SPOT THE CHARACTERS FROM THESE CLASSIC NURSERY RHYMES?

## Little Bo Peep

Little Bo Peep
has lost her sheep
and doesn't know where
to find them.
Leave them alone,
and they'll come home,
wagging their tails
behind them.

## Do You Know the Muffin Man?

Do you know the Muffin Man,
the Muffin Man,
the Muffin Man?
Do you know the Muffin Man
who lives in Drury Lane?

Yes, I know the Muffin Man,
the Muffin Man,
the Muffin Man.
Yes, I know the Muffin Man
who lives in Drury Lane.

## Ring Around the Rosie

Ring around the rosie.
A pocket full of posies.
Ashes! Ashes!
We all fall down.

## Little Boy Blue

Little Boy Blue,
come blow your horn,
the sheep's in the meadow,
the cow's in the corn.
Where is that boy
who looks after the sheep?
Under the haystack
fast asleep.
Will you wake him?
Oh no, not I, for if I do
he will surely cry.

## Baa, Baa, Black Sheep

Baa, baa, black sheep,
have you any wool?
Yes, sir, yes, sir,
three bags full;
one for the master,
and one for the dame,
and one for the little boy
who lives down the lane.

## B-I-N-G-O

There was a farmer had a dog
and Bingo was his name-o.
B-I-N-G-O
B-I-N-G-O
B-I-N-G-O
And Bingo was his name-o.

## London Bridge

London Bridge is falling down,
falling down, falling down.
London Bridge is falling down,
my fair lady.

## Three Little Kittens

Three little kittens,
they lost their mittens,
and they began to cry,
"Oh, mother dear, we sadly fear
our mittens we have lost."
"What! Lost your mittens,
you naughty kittens!
Then you shall have no pie."
"Mee-ow, mee-ow, mee-ow."
"Then, you shall have no pie."

## Where Has My Little Dog Gone?

Where, oh where has
my little dog gone?
Oh where,
oh where can he be?
With his ears so short,
and his tail so long,
oh where,
oh where can he be?

## There Was an Old Woman

There was an old woman
who lived in a shoe.
She had so many children,
she didn't know what to do.
She gave them some broth
without any bread,
then kissed them all soundly
and put them to bed.

## Hey, Diddle Diddle

Hey, diddle diddle,
the cat and the fiddle,
the cow jumped over the moon.
The little dog laughed,
to see such sport,
and the dish ran away
with the spoon.

## There Was a Crooked Man

There was a crooked man,
and he walked a crooked mile.
He found a crooked sixpence
upon a crooked stile.
He bought a crooked cat,
which caught a crooked mouse,
and they all lived together
in a little crooked house.

## To Market, To Market

To market, to market,
to buy a fat pig.
Home again, home again,
jiggety-jig.
To market, to market,
to buy a fat hog.
Home again, home again,
jiggety-jog.

## Little Jack Horner

Little Jack Horner
sat in the corner,
eating a Christmas pie.
He put in his thumb,
and pulled out a plum,
and said,
"What a good boy am I!"

## This Little Piggy

This little piggy went to market.
This little piggy stayed home.
This little piggy had roast beef.
This little piggy had none.
And this little piggy went,
"Whee Whee Whee!"
all the way home.

## Pop! Goes the Weasel

All around the mulberry bush
the monkey chased the weasel.
The monkey thought
'twas all in good sport,
Pop! goes the weasel.

## Shoo, Fly

Shoo, fly, don't bother me!
Shoo, fly, don't bother me!
Shoo, fly, don't bother me,
for I belong to somebody.

## There Was an Old Lady

There was an old lady
who swallowed a fly.
I don't know why
she swallowed a fly.
Perhaps she'll die!
There was an old lady
who swallowed a spider,
that wriggled and wiggled
and tickled inside her.
She swallowed the spider
to catch the fly.
I don't know why
she swallowed a fly.
Perhaps she'll die!

## The Farmer in the Dell

The farmer in the dell,
the farmer in the dell,
heigh-ho, the derry-o,
the farmer in the dell.
The farmer takes a wife,
the farmer takes a wife,
heigh-ho, the derry-o,
the farmer takes a wife.

## Three Blind Mice

Three blind mice,
three blind mice.
See how they run,
see how they run.
They all ran after
the farmer's wife,
who cut off their tails
with a carving knife.
Did you ever see
such a sight in your life,
as three blind mice?

## Row Row Row Your Boat

Row, row, row your boat,
gently down the stream.
Merrily, merrily, merrily, merrily,
life is but a dream.

## Hickory Dickory Dock

Hickory, dickory, dock.
The mouse ran up the clock.
The clock struck one,
the mouse ran down.
Hickory, dickory, dock.

## Simple Simon

Simple Simon
met a pieman,
going to the fair.
Says Simple Simon
to the pieman,
"Let me taste your ware."
Says the pieman
to Simple Simon,
"Show me first your penny."
Says Simple Simon
to the pieman,
"Indeed I have not any."

## Sing a Song of Sixpence

Sing a song of sixpence,
a pocket full of rye.
Four and twenty blackbirds
baked in a pie.
When the pie was opened,
the birds began to sing,
"Wasn't that a dainty dish,
to set before the king?"

## Old King Cole

Old King Cole
was a merry old soul,
and a merry old soul was he.
He called for his pipe,
and he called for his bowl,
and he called for his
fiddlers three.

## Jack Be Nimble

Jack be nimble,
Jack be quick,
Jack jump over
the candlestick.

## The Itsy Bitsy Spider

The itsy bitsy spider
went up the waterspout.
Down came the rain
and washed the spider out.
Out came the sun
and dried up all the rain,
and the itsy bitsy spider
went up the spout again.

## Skip to My Lou

Lou, Lou, skip to my Lou!
Lou, Lou, skip to my Lou!
Lou, Lou, skip to my Lou!
Skip to my Lou, my darling!

Fly's in the buttermilk, shoo, fly, shoo!
Fly's in the buttermilk, shoo, fly, shoo!
Fly's in the buttermilk, shoo, fly, shoo!
Skip to my Lou, my darling!

Lost my partner, what'll I do?
Lost my partner, what'll I do?
Lost my partner, what'll I do?
Skip to my Lou, my darling!

## Pat-a-Cake

Pat-a-cake, pat-a-cake,
baker's man.
Bake me a cake
as fast as you can.
Pat it and shape it
and mark it with "B."
And put it in the oven
for baby and me.

## Humpty Dumpty

Humpty Dumpty
sat on a wall.
Humpty Dumpty
had a great fall.
All the king's horses
and all the king's men
couldn't put Humpty
together again.

## Mary Had a Little Lamb

Mary had a little lamb,
its fleece was white as snow,
and everywhere
that Mary went,
the lamb was sure to go.

## Georgie Porgie

Georgie Porgie,
puddin' and pie,
kissed the girls
and made them cry.
When the boys
came out to play
Georgie Porgie
ran away.

## Little Miss Muffet

Little Miss Muffet
sat on a tuffet,
eating her curds
and whey.
Along came a spider,
who sat down beside her,
and frightened
Miss Muffet away.

## Pease Porridge Hot

Pease porridge hot,
pease porridge cold,
pease porridge in the pot,
nine days old.
Some like it hot,
some like it cold,
some like it in the pot,
nine days old.

## Mary, Mary, Quite Contrary

Mary, Mary, quite contrary,
how does your garden grow?
With silver bells, and cockle shells,
and pretty maids all in a row.

## Jack and Jill

Jack and Jill
went up the hill
to fetch a pail of water.
Jack fell down
and broke his crown,
and Jill came tumbling after.

## Little Robin Redbreast

Little Robin Redbreast
sat upon a tree.
Up went the Pussy Cat,
and down went he.
Down came Pussy Cat,
away Robin ran.
Says little Robin Redbreast,
"Catch me if you can!"

## Wee Willie Winkie

Wee Willie Winkie
runs through the town,
upstairs and downstairs
in his nightgown.
Rapping at the window,
crying at the lock,
"Are the children
in their beds,
for now it's eight o'clock?"

## Rub-A-Dub-Dub

Rub-a-dub-dub,
three men in a tub,
and who do you think
they were?
The butcher, the baker,
the candlestick maker,
and all of them gone
to the fair!

For my three bears,
You are my greatest adventure. —A.L.W.

**LITTLE BO PEEP AND HER BAD, BAD SHEEP © 2016 BY CAPSTONE YOUNG READERS.**

Published by Capstone Young Readers in 2016. 1710 Roe Crest Drive, North Mankato, MN 56003 · www.mycapstone.com

Cataloging-in-Publication Data is available on the Library of Congress website.

ISBN 978-1-62370-501-5 (paper over board)  ISBN 978-1-62370-612-8 (ebook pdf)

Book design by Bob Lentz

Printed in the United States of America in North Mankato, Minnesota.
052016   009742R